HENRY HECKELBECK

and the Haunted Hideout

By **Wanda Coven**

Illustrated by **Priscilla Burris**

LITTLE SIMON

New York London Toronto Sydney New Delhi

This book is a work of fiction. Any references to historical events, real people, or real places are used fictitiously. Other names, characters, places, and events are products of the author's imagination, and any resemblance to actual events or places or persons, living or dead, is entirely coincidental.

LITTLE SIMON
An imprint of Simon & Schuster Children's Publishing Division
1230 Avenue of the Americas, New York, New York 10020
First Little Simon paperback edition July 2020
Copyright © 2020 by Simon & Schuster, Inc.
Also available in a Little Simon hardcover edition.
All rights reserved, including the right of reproduction in whole or in part in any form. LITTLE SIMON is a registered trademark of Simon & Schuster, Inc., and associated colophon is a trademark of Simon & Schuster, Inc.
For information about special discounts for bulk purchases, please contact Simon & Schuster Special Sales at 1-866-506-1949 or business@simonandschuster.com. The Simon & Schuster Speakers Bureau can bring authors to your live event. For more information or to book an event contact the Simon & Schuster Speakers Bureau at 1-866-248-3049 or visit our website at www.simonspeakers.com.
Designed by Leslie Mechanic
Manufactured in the United States of America 0321 MTN
10 9 8 7 6 5 4 3
This book is cataloged with the Library of Congress.
ISBN 978-1-5344-6117-8 (hc)
ISBN 978-1-5344-6116-1 (pbk)
ISBN 978-1-5344-6118-5 (eBook)

CONTENTS

Chapter 1

BACKYARD SPIES

Dudley Day whispered, "I spy an anthill!"

Henry Heckelbeck joined his best friend to watch the ants. They both wondered if the ants had secret tunnels inside.

"I spy a bird's nest!" cried Henry, pointing his binoculars at the treetops. "Wouldn't a nest make a cool hangout?"

Dudley stood up and said, "Yeah. So would an anthill."

Then Henry spotted a red-orange cat in the garden.

"I spy something FURRY," he whispered. The cat belonged to the next-door neighbors. Henry had nicknamed him Kevin.

Dudley tiptoed to Henry's side. "Let's follow it!" he said.

The boys tracked Kevin along
the stone wall and down into
Henry's dad's vegetable patch.
Kevin stopped and chewed on
some spinach.

"Ew!" the boys cried.

Then Kevin trotted toward the house and leaped onto a windowsill.

The boys crouched under the window. They slowly stood up to spy on the cat, but Kevin bounded away.

Now the only things in the window were Henry and Dudley.

Henry could see his sister, Heidi. She was inside the house with her friends Bruce Bickerson and Lucy Lancaster. Then Heidi saw Henry.

"HEY!" she shouted at her brother. "Quit SPYING on us!"

Henry and Dudley ran away before they got blamed for anything else Kevin did.

Chapter 2

ON A MISSION

"What WE need is a space of our own!" Henry declared.

Dudley nodded. "Someplace where nobody can bug us!"

The boys had a new mission: Secret Hideout Search.

First they tried behind the
bushes in Henry's backyard.

"Not roomy enough," Henry
said.

Next they checked behind
the fence, but a grapevine was
in the way.

"Look over here," said Dudley. He led Henry under the branches of a pine tree.

Then they heard Heidi yelling from inside the house.

"I can STILL see you!" she shouted.

"Merg," said Henry. "Let's get out of here."

The boys got permission to go to Charmed Court Park down the street. They raced all the way there.

"Hey, let's look inside that hedge!" Dudley suggested.

The boys slid sideways into the middle of the hedge. It was nice and roomy inside—a perfect place for a hideout, except for one thing. They had crossed into squirrel territory.

"*Kuk! Kuk! Kuk!*" an angry squirrel scolded, and it charged at them.

"*AAAAAAAH!*" squealed the boys as they scrambled out of the hedge.

"Forget THAT!" Henry said.

Dudley brushed off his shirt and asked, "Now what do we do?"

Henry thought for a moment. "Now we race to the top of the climbing wall at the playground!" he said. "Ready? GO!"

The boys dashed to the wall and climbed up like daddy longlegs.

"WE TIED!" Henry shouted when they reached the top at the same time. Then they peered into the opening where the three walls connected.

"Look down there!" Dudley said, pointing to the space below. "That would make a GREAT hideout!"

The boys hopped down into the space.

"Wow, this place is like an anthill, only for KIDS!" Dudley exclaimed.

Henry leaned his head against the wall. "And best of all, Heidi will NEVER find us in here!"

Chapter 3

WHO GOES THERE?

The next day the boys spied somebody reading a book in their secret No-Heidi Hideout.

"WHO GOES THERE?" Henry shouted. "And you better not be my sister!"

It was Max Maplethorpe, the new girl in Henry and Dudley's class.

"It's ME," said Max.

Both of the boys wrinkled their noses.

"You DARE to invade our secret hideout?" Dudley asked.

Max frowned and said, "This place is no secret."

The boys sighed heavily and lowered themselves into the den.

"Secret hideouts are sure hard to come by," Henry complained.

"You're not kidding," said Max as she pointed to the  opening at the top. The boys looked up and saw lots of little kids peering down at them.

"Oh no!" cried Henry. "MORE
invaders! Now we have to find
another hideout!"

Chapter 4

THE MAGIC SEED

By dinnertime the boys hadn't found anything.

Henry went home and flopped onto his bed. He felt something weird under his pillow. It was that old book!

He stared at the cover, and it opened up *by itself*! Then the medallion inside floated right out of the book!

The chain circled around Henry's head and gently came to rest around his neck. Pages in the book fluttered and stopped on a spell that Henry read over.

How to Plant a Secret Hideout

Have you ever wanted a private space to hide out with your friends? Perhaps you'd like to get away from an annoying sibling or snoopy kids in general? Well, if you're in need of a secret hideout, then this spell is for you!

Ingredients:
1 secret wish, written down
2 left-footed socks
1 pair of sunglasses
1 mirror

Mix the ingredients together in a bowl. Then hold your hand palm-side up to receive a magic seed. Chant the following spell:

A nest! A lair! A cubbyhole!
A place for friends to go.
Grant me now a hidey-hole!
A seed that I can sow!

Note: Plant the seed wherever you want your hideout. The hideout will only be visible to you and your friends.

Henry quickly wrote down
his wish:

One
AWESOME
hideout

Then he grabbed two socks
from his dresser, a pair of
sunglasses from his beach bag,
and a toy mirror from Heidi's
pretend makeup kit.

one AWESOME hideout

33

34

Henry mixed the ingredients together and chanted the spell. A burst of sparkles shimmered over the bowl, and then a magic seed appeared in his hand.

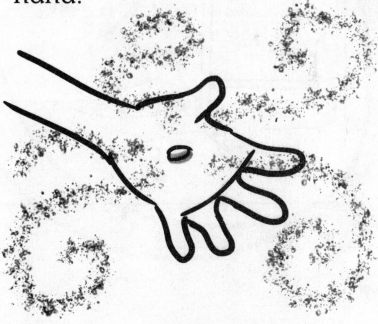

Chapter 5

WHOOPS!

Henry clutched the seed in his fist. *Now I need to find the PERFECT secret hideout spot!*

He ran to the playroom. Heidi twirled on the swing that hung from the ceiling.

Not in here! he thought.

Henry circled through the dining room, the kitchen, and the den. *Mom would never allow a hideout in any of THESE rooms,* he thought.

Henry kept going until he found Heidi again! She was lying on the sofa.

"Not YOU again!" she sneered.

Henry stuck out his tongue and disappeared into the backyard. *Maybe I'll plant the hideout somewhere sneaky,* he thought.

Then Kevin the cat trotted over. Henry knelt down to say hello, but Kevin jumped into Henry's lap.

Henry lost his balance and dropped the magic seed—right in the middle of the yard.

"Oh no!" Henry cried as Kevin scampered away. "Not HERE!"

But it was too late. The seed instantly grew into a giant round bush.

"Now EVERYONE will know where my secret hideout is!" Henry grumbled.

Then Henry remembered something: The hideout would only be visible to him and his friends.

Henry quickly found the opening and climbed inside.

"WHOA!" he cried. "This place is COOL-O NOOL-O!"

The magic hideout had lots of space and a thick web of branches all around. There was even enough sunlight to play games or do homework. It was perfect!

Then Henry heard his
mother calling him for dinner.
He left the hideout and ran
all the way to the house.

Before he opened the back door, he turned around to make *sure* the secret hideout was really there.

And sure enough, it *really* was.

Chapter 6

WHAT WAS THAT?

The next day Henry showed Dudley the secret hideout.

"How did we miss this?!" Dudley exclaimed. "Has this bush been here all along?"

Henry thought fast.

"Uh, no," he said. "We JUST got this bush!"

Dudley bought it. "Well, it's totally cool!"

The boys climbed in and set up their stuff.

"Guess what I brought?" Dudley said as he pulled opened his backpack.

Henry rubbed his hands together and guessed, "Hmm, is it something to eat?"

Dudley nodded. "Bananas! Brownies! And chips!"

One by one he laid out the snacks. Dudley took a brownie, and Henry chose a banana.

While they were munching, they heard a strange sound in the branches above them.

"What in the world is that noise?" whispered Dudley.

Henry shook his head. "I don't know," he said, his heart beating faster.

The boys sat very still and listened. Something rustled inside the branches.

The leaves shook. Then, all at once, the entire bush began to shake.

The boys squealed. Then they pushed and shoved each other out of the hideout. They sat on the ground and caught their breath.

"Maybe Heidi's pranking us,"
said Henry.

The boys searched the entire
backyard. They didn't see Heidi
anywhere.

When the spooky feelings had worn off, the boys crawled back into the hideout.

"Seems normal now," Henry said.

Dudley nodded and picked up his joke book to read.

Henry decided to finish his banana. He pulled back the rest of the peel, but the banana was all gone.

"That's weird," Henry said. "I thought I had a little banana left."

Dudley looked up from his joke book. "That IS weird. Because you know what ghosts love to eat?"

Henry shrugged.

Dudley smiled and yelled, "BOO-nanas!"

Chapter 7

NOT AGAIN!

For a week the hideout stayed as normal as a magic hideout could be. Henry was sitting inside with his spy notebook, when a hand pulled back the branches.

It was Dudley, but he wasn't alone. Max was with him.

"Uh, hi, Henry," Dudley mumbled. "I kinda, sorta ran into Max and kinda, sorta told her about your hideout, and she kinda, sorta wanted to see it."

Max looked over Dudley's shoulder. "And the little kids at the rock-climbing wall wouldn't leave me alone. I just want a quiet place to hang out."

Henry knew what *that* felt like.

"Okay, sure. Come in," he said.

"This place is spectacular!"
Max said as she entered. "It's
like a dome made of branches!"

Henry smiled. He was very
proud of his magical hideout.

The three friends settled in.
Max read her book, and Henry
and Dudley went over their
spy notes from school.

"Did you know Principal

Pennypacker had a cream-cheese-and-olive sandwich for lunch today?" Henry asked.

Dudley scrunched his nose. "That's gross."

Henry nodded. "And did
you know the water fountain
overflowed today?" he asked.
"I reported it to Mr. Fortini."

66

"What caused it?" Dudley
asked.

"Bubble gum."

Dudley made a note of it.

Suddenly the rustling began
again. Max set down her
book. The three friends froze
and stared into the branches.

Then—*SHOOP!*—Max's book slid across the floor by itself. The kids squished themselves into the corner.

"Guys, is this a prank?" Max whispered. "Because it isn't funny!"

Henry and Dudley stared at Max with huge owl eyes.

"We're not doing anything," Henry whispered.

Then Dudley pointed at Max's head. "Max, does your baseball cap normally float above your head?"

Max looked up at her floating hat and screamed.

The kids darted out of the hideout as fast as possible and tumbled onto the lawn, gasping for breath.

Max was the first to speak. "Guys!" she cried. "Your hideout is TOTALLY HAUNTED!"

Chapter 8

GHOST ZAPPER

Max dusted herself off and put her hat back on.

"Today is your lucky day to have a haunted hideout," she told the boys, "because I am an expert ghost zapper!"

Henry and Dudley looked at each other.

"A WHAT?" they asked.

Max helped them up. "I know how to remove ghosts. We had some in our old garage that made the same exact noises as your ghost. Do you want to know why?"

Henry and Dudley nodded.

"YOU are in the ghost's personal space," she told them. "Would you like help getting rid of the ghost?"

The boys nodded again.

"Okay, let's go!" Max cried as she climbed back into the hideout. "All you have to do is follow my directions."

The boys carefully went in after her.

Max called out to the ghost.
"Oh, Ghost! Tell us your
demands!"

Immediately, the bush
shook. Henry

and Dudley
grabbed hold
of each other.

"Now that we have the ghost's attention, we can begin," explained Max. "First you have to clap loudly."

The boys let go of each other and began to clap as loudly as they could.

Max nodded. "Now stomp your feet at the same time and move in a circle!"

The boys did as Max said.
"Very good!" she said. "Now
cluck like a chicken."

The boys clapped, stomped, and clucked in a circle.

"Cluck even LOUDER!" Max demanded.

The boys clucked louder.

"Wow, that's REALLY good!" Max said. "Now you have to ACT like a ghost!"

The boys held their arms out and began to moan and groan.

Max looked up at the branches. "It's WORKING!"

The boys kept at it until Max held up her hand like a stop sign.

"YOU DID IT! The ghost is GONE!"

Both of the boys stopped and listened. They didn't hear any rustling.

But they did hear another
sound. It was the sound of
Max laughing her head off.

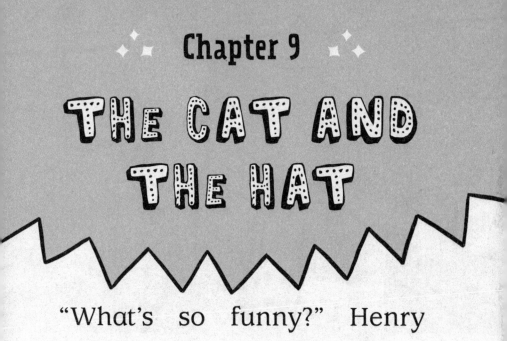

Chapter 9
THE CAT AND THE HAT

"What's so funny?" Henry asked.

"YOU ARE!" Max roared.

Henry and Dudley didn't understand.

"Don't you get it?" said Max.

"There never WAS a ghost!"

Both boys folded their arms.

"You mean we acted like chickens for no reason?" Dudley asked.

Max fell to the ground laughing. "YUP! And you should have seen yourselves!"

The boys watched in disbelief.

"Then who made all those creepy rustling sounds?" asked Henry.

"I'll show you!" said Max.

Then she clicked her tongue
and   rubbed   two   fingers
together.

Soon a furry face poked
through the branches.
It was *Kevin*!

"Here's your 'ghost'!" Max declared. "I saw him when I got here. I thought you knew he was hiding. When you jumped at the rustling sounds, I decided to play a prank on you!"

Henry and Dudley both screamed about being so silly.

"Wow, you totally GOT US!" said Henry.

Then they all burst out laughing.

"But how did your book slide across the floor?" Dudley asked.

"The cat batted it away, and it went flying!" said Max. "The same with my cap. The cat lifted it off my head with its claws."

Henry and Dudley shook their heads. It had been the perfect prank. And the boys *loved* pranks—even when the prank was on them.

Dudley scooped up Kevin into his arms. "You are a little troublemaker!" he said, rubbing his cheek on Kevin's fur.

Then Dudley let out a giant sneeze. Then another, and another, and another!

"Uh-oh. Are you allergic to cats?" asked Max.

Dudley sniffled and said, "Maybe I am!"

They put Kevin outside—
even though Henry knew
perfectly well Kevin would
come right back in.

"Well, it looks like we need
to find another new hideout,"
Henry announced.

Chapter 10

UP A TREE

This time Henry and Dudley wanted a tree house. There was a perfect tree in Dudley's backyard. Henry's dad agreed to help them build it on one condition: The kids had to help.

Dad created the plans on his computer. Then they picked out wood at the lumberyard. Dad did most of the carpentry. Henry helped build the ladder.

Dudley and Max collected things to furnish the tree house. Max brought four foam chairs from her house.

Dudley brought a rug. And Henry found a round table in the basement.

Dad installed three windows
in the hideout. He placed pegs
on the wall to hang jackets
and spy gear. He also made
a special trapdoor entrance to
keep out critters.

"There's no way Kevin can
get in now!" Dudley said.

Henry shared a look with Max. They both knew cats can climb almost anywhere, but they didn't share that with Dudley.

When the tree house was done, the friends hung a sign on the outside that read:

Then they sat on the comfy foam chairs and had their first official secret hideout meeting.

As they talked, a pebble ticked off the side of the tree house.

Henry peeked out one of the windows.

It was Heidi and her friends Lucy and Bruce.

"Hey there, my favorite little brother," Heidi said sweetly. "Can we come over for a visit? Please?"

Henry smirked because he was Heidi's *only* little brother. Still, he really wanted to show off their new hideout.

"Sure," he said. "I have to warn you, though. . . . They say this place is haunted."

Haunted by a cat named Kevin, thought Henry. *But Heidi and her friends don't need to know that. Mwoo-hoo-haa-haa-haa!*

Henry Heckelbeck opened his spy notebook.

"Got any NEW secret INFO?" he asked.

Henry's best friend, Dudley Day, lowered his spyglass.

"Yup, see that kid on the kickball field? The one at home plate?"

Henry nodded.

"Well, that kid USUALLY kicks with his RIGHT foot," Dudley explained. "But watch closely."

Henry watched the boy kick the ball.

"Whoa, he just kicked with his LEFT! Good one, Dudster."

An excerpt from *Henry Heckelbeck Spells Trouble*

Henry made a note of it. Then he shared something he had spied. "Did you see that third grader who got a buzz cut? Now you can see where his tan line stops!"

Dudley laughed. "He has a racing stripe on his neck!"

Henry jotted down *racing stripe*.

"And you know what else?" Henry said.

An excerpt from *Henry Heckelbeck Spells Trouble*